Hol Ch

We hope you enjoy this book.
Please return or renew it by the due date.
You can renew it at **www.norfolk.gov.uk/libraries**
or by using our free library app. Otherwise you can
phone **0344 800 8020** - please have your library
card and pin ready.
You can sign up for email reminders too.

GR  KEY

NORFOLK COUNTY COUNCIL
LIBRARY AND INFORMATION SERVICE

NORFOLK ITEM

3 0129 08825 0965

PUFFIN BOOKS

UK | USA | Canada | Ireland | Australia | India | New Zealand | South Africa

Puffin Books is part of the Penguin Random House group of companies whose
addresses can be found at global.penguinrandomhouse.com.

www.penguin.co.uk   www.puffin.co.uk   www.ladybird.co.uk

Penguin
Random House
UK

First published in the USA by Random House Children's Books 2018
This edition published in the UK by Puffin Books 2023
001
Text copyright © Suzanne Lang, 2018
Illustrations copyright © Max Lang, 2018
The moral right of the author and illustrator has been asserted

Printed in China

A CIP catalogue record for this book is available from the British Library

ISBN: 978–0–241–62869–0

All correspondence to:
Puffin Books, Penguin Random House Children's
One Embassy Gardens, 8 Viaduct Gardens
London SW11 7BW

For our parents — S.L. and M.L.

GRUMPY MONKEY

By Suzanne Lang

Illustrated by Max Lang

PUFFIN

One wonderful day, Jim Panzee woke to discover that nothing was right.

The sun was too bright, the sky was too blue and the bananas were too sweet.

Jim was confused.

"What's going on?"

"Maybe you're grumpy," suggested
Norman from next door.

"I'm not grumpy!" Jim insisted.

On his walk, he met Marabou.

"Jim's grumpy," Norman told Marabou.

"Why are you grumpy, Jim?" asked Marabou.

"It's such a wonderful day."

"Grumpy! Me? I'm not grumpy," said Jim.

"But look at how you're standing," Marabou said.

"It's true," said Norman. "You're all hunched."

So Jim loosened up.

Then he ran into Lemur.

"Jim's grumpy," Norman told Lemur.

"Why are you grumpy, Jim?" asked Lemur.

"It's such a wonderful day."

"Grumpy! Me? I'm not grumpy," said Jim.

"Your eyebrows look grumpy," said Lemur.

"It's true," said Norman. "They're all bunched up."

So Jim raised his brow.

Then he tripped over Snake.

"Oh no," said Norman. "That's the last thing you need when you're feeling so grumpy."

"Grumpy! Me? I'm not grumpy," said Jim.

"Then why that frown?" said Snake.

"I think it's because he tripped over you,"
Norman whispered to Snake.

So Jim put on a smile.

Finally, Jim looked happy.

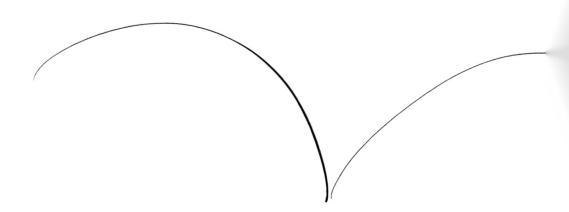

But he didn't feel happy inside.

Everyone wanted Jim to enjoy this wonderful day.

"You should sing with us!" said the birds.

Jim didn't feel like singing.

"You should swing with us!"
said the monkeys.
Jim didn't feel like swinging.

"You should roll with us!" said the zebras.

Jim didn't feel like rolling.

"You should stroll with us!" said the peacocks.

Jim didn't feel like strolling.

"You should lie in the grass!"

"You should stomp your feet!"

"You should take a bath!"

"And make a splash!"

"You should hug someone!"

"You should laugh!

"You should take a nap!"

"You should eat old meat!"

"Or some honey!"

"You should jump up and down!"

"You should sit in the sun!"

"You should dance!"

But Jim didn't feel like doing any of that.

"Why are you grumpy, Jim?" asked the others. "It's such a wonderful day."

I'M NOT GRUMPY!

shouted Jim as he beat his chest.

And he stormed off.

Jim felt sorry. A little sorry for shouting at
everyone, but mostly sorry for himself.

"I guess I am grumpy," Jim sighed.

And just as he was starting to feel really sad . . .

. . . he came upon Norman. Norman was slumped. His eyebrows were bunched up, and he was frowning.

"What's the matter? Are you grumpy?" asked Jim.

"No. I danced with Porcupine," said Norman.

"Are you OK?" asked Jim.

"It hurts, but I'll probably feel better soon enough," said Norman. "Are you still grumpy?"

"Yes," said Jim, "but I'll probably feel better soon enough, too. For now, I need to be grumpy."

"It's a wonderful day to be grumpy," said Norman.

Jim agreed.

And he already felt a little bit better.